Too Young for Yiddish

Richard Michelson • Illustrated by Neil Waldman

TALEWINDS

A Charlesbridge Imprint

For Samuel and Esther, Abraham and Ida, and the whole mishpocheh
—R. M.

To Monica Woolf and the students of Beth Yeshurun School.
—N. W.

Text copyright © 2002 by Richard Michelson
Illustrations copyright © 2002 by Neil Waldman

A **TALEWINDS** Book
Published by Charlesbridge Publishing
85 Main Street, Watertown, MA 02472
(617) 926-0329
www.charlesbridge.com

Library of Congress Cataloging-in-Publication Data
Michelson, Richard.
Too young for yiddish/Richard Michelson; illustrated by Neil Waldman.
p.   cm.
"A Talewinds Book"
Summary: When Aaron was a small boy his Grandpa, or Zayde, would not teach him Yiddish, but as an adult,
Aaron longs to learn the language and history of the Old Country from Zayde and his many books.
ISBN 0-88106-118-2 (reinforced for library use)
[1. Yiddish language—Fiction. 2. Grandfathers—Fiction. 3. Jews—United States—Fiction.
4. Language and languages—Fiction.] I. Waldman, Neil, ill. II. Title.
PZ7.M581915 To 2001
[E]—dc21   00-064859

Printed in China
(hc) 10 9 8 7 6 5 4 3 2 1

Illustrations in this book done in watercolor and pen on Arches hot press watercolor paper
Display type and text type set in Centaur
Color separations by Sung In Printing, South Korea
Printed and bound in China by Everbest Printing Co. Ltd through Four Colour Imports Ltd, Louisville, Kentucky
Production supervision by Brian G. Walker
Designed by Diane M. Earley

Editor's Note

Yiddish books are printed "back to front" and read right to left. While we didn't print the text right to left, *Too Young for Yiddish* is bound "back to front" to share an aspect of Yiddish culture with you.

Interested in learning more about preserving the Yiddish language? Check out the National Yiddish Book Center's Web site:
http://www.yiddishbookcenter.org

All afternoon Aaron helped carry—or *shlep*, as his grandpa, Zayde, called it—boxes of books up the apartment-house stairs. Bubbeh, Aaron's grandma, had died less than a month ago, and now Zayde was going to share Aaron's own small room.

"Papa," Aaron's father complained, "the room is tiny. Too many books!"

But Zayde just waved his hand and opened the top dresser drawer. "The highest for *di poetn*," he said. Then he filled drawers two and three with stories and plays. In the bottom drawer he folded his underwear, two pairs of pants, three shirts, his *tefillin*, and a stack of clean white handkerchiefs. His prayer shawl he draped over the back of the one wooden chair.

"*Haym*," he said, smiling. "Home." And he gave Aaron a big *hartzig* hug.

So many books. Had Zayde really read them all?
Each with its own ideas and mysteries. Each with its
own secret world. Aaron opened a drawer to take a
closer look. He lifted out one book and then another.
But he could not read a single word. They were all
written in a language he did not understand.

Aaron's mother said that Zayde spoke Yiddish in the
Old Country, although Aaron wasn't exactly sure where
the Old Country was.

"In my village no one spoke English," Zayde told him.
"The *shochet*—our kosher butcher—would sing to the
chickens in Yiddish, '*Sholem aleichem, hindlekh*'—'Peace,
little chickens'—and the chickens would cluck back in
Yiddish, '*Aleichem sholem, shochet.*'"

"And the children," Aaron asked, "did they all
speak Yiddish, too?"

"Of course," Zayde answered. "The children, too."

"Then teach me Yiddish," Aaron begged, "so I, too,
can talk to the chickens."

Zayde laughed. "Oy, *tateleh*, you are too young for Yiddish. In the Old Country things were different. Jews kept to themselves. We were forced into ghettos and forbidden to play with the other children. But America is like soup. Everyone mixes together. Here Jewish boys can play baseball just like everyone else. And here Jews should speak English just like everyone else."

Aaron didn't argue. He had to admit that he was a little bit embarrassed by Zayde's funny accent and the way he waved his arms when he spoke.

That summer the Brooklyn Dodgers won the pennant. Aaron wanted to be a pitcher, just like Brooklyn-born Sandy Koufax, his new favorite player. He loved to talk to Zayde about ERAs and RBIs and the difference between a spitball and a slider.

Zayde listened, but he didn't understand a single word. "Such a language," he said, laughing. "You are too young for Yiddish, and I am too old to talk baseball." But together they sat and listened to every pitch of every game of the World Series.

What a celebration when the Dodgers won! Aaron jumped up and down, and even Zayde waved his arms and yelled, "*Mazel tov!*" at the final pitch.

Life was good and about to get better. Aaron's father had gotten a new job in the suburbs. Soon they would all move to a bigger house. "Such huge rooms," he said. "A den with a bookcase for Papa. And for you, Aaron, a front yard to play catch in."

But Zayde ruined everything. He decided to stay behind.

"In the Old Country," Zayde said, "Jews could not get good jobs. Children were forbidden to attend *cheder*. Our houses and our books were burned. My parents packed and moved plenty. Too many times we traveled from town to town in search of a better life. But here I'm already happy. I have friends from the Old Country. We speak the same language."

Zayde grew quiet. He stopped waving his arms, and then he put them around Aaron. "Besides," he said, his eyes twinkling, "soon you will be busy with your studies. Too busy to *shmooz* with an old man all day."

The next morning Zayde rented a room at Mr. Singer's Home for the Aged. The front hall was full of *bubbehs* and *zaydes* reading and chatting and playing chess. Mr. Grayson, the grocer, had saved some extra boxes, and Aaron filled each one with Zayde's books. Now he *shlepped* them up three flights of stairs.

Mr. Singer shook his head and made a clicking sound with his tongue so that it seemed as if his head rattled. "Oy, Aaron, what are we to do with your *zayde*? Here our hearts are big, but the rooms are tiny. Too many books!"

But Aaron just waved his hand and opened Zayde's top dresser drawer.

The years passed, and Aaron studied hard, just as Zayde had predicted. He spent hours and hours in the library. So many books. Each with its own secret world.

Books in French and English and Spanish.

Books about world wars and kings and knights in shining armor.

Books about foreign lands and fearless explorers.

But every chance he got, Aaron took the train back to Brooklyn and visited Zayde. He told him about Sandy Koufax and how he had refused to pitch on Yom Kippur. He told him about the Dodgers and how they had moved all the way across the country to Los Angeles. "But to me," Aaron said, "they will always be the Brooklyn Dodgers. Brooklyn is where they came from. No one can change that."

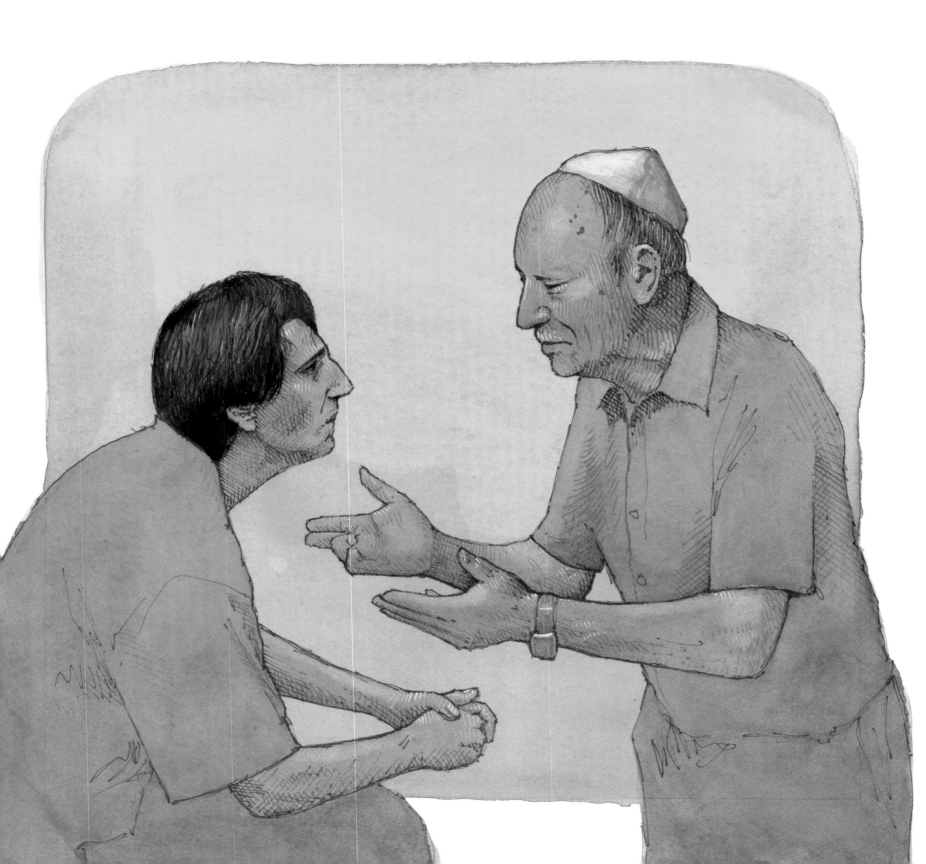

But some things do change. Aaron graduated from high school, and Zayde grew old. Too old even for Mr. Singer's. It was time to move to a nursing home.

"Don't worry, Zayde," Aaron told him, "I'll pack your books."

"Oy, *tateleh*," Zayde sighed. "Why *shlep*? In the nursing home the rooms are tiny. Besides, I can barely see anymore, and my friends from the Old Country are already with God. I, myself, called the janitor this morning." Zayde pointed out the window, and a chill crept up Aaron's spine.

There, spilling out of bags and trash bins, heaped on the curb across from Aaron's car, lay all of Zayde's precious books. Whole worlds piled high like worthless rags.

Zayde's voice trembled. "In America," he said, "the soup has lost its flavor. Everyone has mixed too well. No one remembers anymore where they came from. For Yiddish it is the bottom of the ninth, with two outs and no one on base."

Then Zayde smiled. "*Oy, gevalt!* Listen to me. I guess you're never too old to talk baseball."

"In that case," Aaron said, leaning over to give Zayde a big *hartzig* hug, "it's time you taught me to talk to the chickens." With that, Aaron straightened up and strode out of the room. Zayde heard Aaron's footsteps on the stairs and saw him bound down Mr. Singer's front stoop. He watched as Aaron opened his car doors, stacking in stories and plays until even the trunk was overflowing. Only when the last book of poems was piled neatly on the front passenger seat did Aaron look up. Through the window he could see Zayde waving, his arms moving every which way.

Letter by letter, word by word, Aaron learned Zayde's language. Once each week he *shlepped* an armful of books up the nursing home stairs. Together they recited poems by Zayde's favorite poets. Aaron loved to hear the rhythms that rolled off Zayde's tongue. Sometimes the stories they read together made Aaron laugh and cry at the same time. And sometimes the stories they read together reminded Zayde of a story of his own.

He told Aaron all about the *shtetl* in Eastern Europe where he fed his family's chickens, chopped wood, and studied Torah. Once Zayde even mimicked his mother's accent and the way she waved her arms when she spoke. Aaron could almost hear the *tummel* of the marketplace where his great-grandmother bargained for bread and books and shoes.

"So long ago," Zayde insisted, "that the World Series wasn't even invented yet. Of course," and now Zayde stopped joking, "we Jews had little time for play. We were poor and lived always like visitors on someone else's home field. When times turned bad, it was we who were blamed. There were *pogroms,* and Jews were pulled into the streets and beaten."

"And the children," Aaron asked, "did they suffer, too?"

"Of course," Zayde whispered, "the children, too."

Aaron had studied hard in school, but he'd never realized before how little he knew of his own *zayde*'s life. For the first time he understood that history was what happened to real people, and he learned how easily families could be torn apart. Zayde had kissed his family good-bye forever, at an age younger than Aaron was now.

"Remember us," Zayde's mother had whispered, "in your prayers."

"And I knew from my *tateh*'s tears," Zayde remembered, "that we would never see each other again. But my parents wanted more for me than a life of poverty. In America, they'd heard, Jews could study and find jobs and live just like everyone else." Zayde smiled. "Or just maybe, they knew that in America I would meet your *bubbeh*."

And years later, after Zayde, too, had met his God, Aaron told Zayde's stories to his own son. He had named him Samuel, which had been Zayde's name and the name of Zayde's *zayde*.

"That way," Aaron told him, "you will always remember where you came from. No one can change that."

"Then teach me Yiddish," Samuel begged, "so I, too, can talk to the chickens."

"Oy, *tataleh*," Aaron said, laughing. "*Zol zein azoy*, let it be so. You are never too young for Yiddish."

About the Yiddish Language

Yiddish, a mixture of primarily German, Polish, and Hebrew, was the everyday language spoken by three-quarters of the world's Jews for over one thousand years. Hebrew, with its exalted cadences, remained the language of choice for prayer. With its earthy rhythms, by turns sarcastic and sentimental tone, and wit and passion, Yiddish mirrored the daily life of the Diaspora (those Jews living outside of Palestine, their traditional homeland). But between 1939 and 1945, Hitler and the Nazis virtually wiped out the Yiddish language and the culture that spoke it. Six million Jews were murdered in Nazi death camps.

Many Jews who escaped to the Soviet Union were later slaughtered by Stalin. As part of his anti-Jewish campaign, Stalin ordered the execution of his country's major Yiddish writers and intellectuals on the single night of August 12, 1952.

Those Jews who escaped to Palestine, modern-day Israel, adopted Hebrew as their everyday language. Yiddish seemed a language of defeat and shame. It was, as the great Yiddish writer Isaac Bashevis Singer often boasted, "a language without a word for weapons." Zionists, Jews intent on founding their own country, felt they needed to look to the future and forget the recent past, so the speaking of Yiddish was suppressed.

In the United States, Yiddish-speaking Jews were welcomed. But these Jews wanted nothing more than to fit in, and they willingly learned the English of their newly adopted country.

Yiddish remained a language without a home. The great Yiddish poets and storytellers seemed consigned to the dustbin of history, their worlds of Jewish wisdom and humor buried with them. Over time, however, as younger generations of Jews began to feel more assimilated, their attitude toward Yiddish began to change. Jews have always relied on historical memory to know who they are, where they came from, and where they might be headed. The Yiddish language provides a crucial link to the ancestors and culture that nourished the Jewish people for more than a thousand years.

Yiddish Words

bubbeh (BUB-eh): grandmother

cheder (KHAY-der): the schoolroom where Torah is studied

di poetn (DEE po-ETN): the poets

gevalt (geh-VAHLT): an exclamation of surprise or dismay

hartzig (HART-zig): heartfelt

haym (HAME): home

hindlekh (HIND-lekh): chickens

mazel tov (MAH-zl TUF): a saying meaning "congratulations" or "thank God!"

oy (OY): a cry of astonishment, such as "Oh, my!"

pogrom (puh-GROM): a massacre of innocent people

shmooz (SHMOOZE): friendly chat

shochet (SHOY-khet): a ritual slaughterer of animals

sholem aleichem (SHOW-lem ah-LAY-khem): a greeting meaning "peace to you"

shlep (SHLEP): to carry

shtetl (SHTET-ul): a little town

tateh (TAH-teh): father

tateleh (TAH-teh-leh): little father; an affectionate way to address a little boy

tefillin (teh-FILL-in): two small leather boxes, worn by Jewish men during morning weekday prayers, that contain slips inscribed with passages from the Bible

tummel (TUM-ul): noisy disorder

Yom Kippur (yom-KIP-per): the Day of Atonement; the most solemn Jewish holiday, marked by fasting and prayer

zayde (ZAY-dee): grandfather

zol zein azoy (ZOLE ZINE a-ZOY): let it be so

Note: Although Yiddish uses the Hebrew alphabet and, like Hebrew, is read from right to left, it is as dissimilar from Hebrew as French is from English. In this book, common English transliterations for the Yiddish words have been used, although there are other variant and equally correct spellings.

Afterword

While the Aaron of this story is a fictional character, his son Samuel might have been taught by the real-life Aaron Lansky.

In 1980 Aaron Lansky, a twenty-three-year-old college student, decided to save Yiddish books. No one else wanted them. The population of older Yiddish speakers was dying, and their children, who could not read these books, had no interest in saving them. "Priceless books were being discarded and destroyed," Aaron recalls, "not by anti-Semites, but by Jews."

Aaron advertised for books. He salvaged them from garages, basements, and trash bins. When they no longer fit in his room, he rented a warehouse. He organized a network of *zamlers*, or collectors, to gather books from all over the world. Scholars had estimated that fewer than 65,000 Yiddish books were still in circulation, but today Aaron has collected over 1,300,000 volumes.

Book collecting, however, is not an end in itself. It is the means to teach young people about the worlds contained within the books so that they can know their own history. More than an exercise in nostalgia, Yiddish is a window through which we can see the Jewish past.

From its beginnings in an unheated factory loft, the National Yiddish Book Center in Amherst, Massachusetts, has become a world-renowned cultural institution. It is a living center where books and educational programs bring the past thousand years alive for a new generation. Its bookshelves are dedicated to *bubbehs* and *zaydes* from around the world. For now, the Yiddish language is no longer in danger of disappearing.